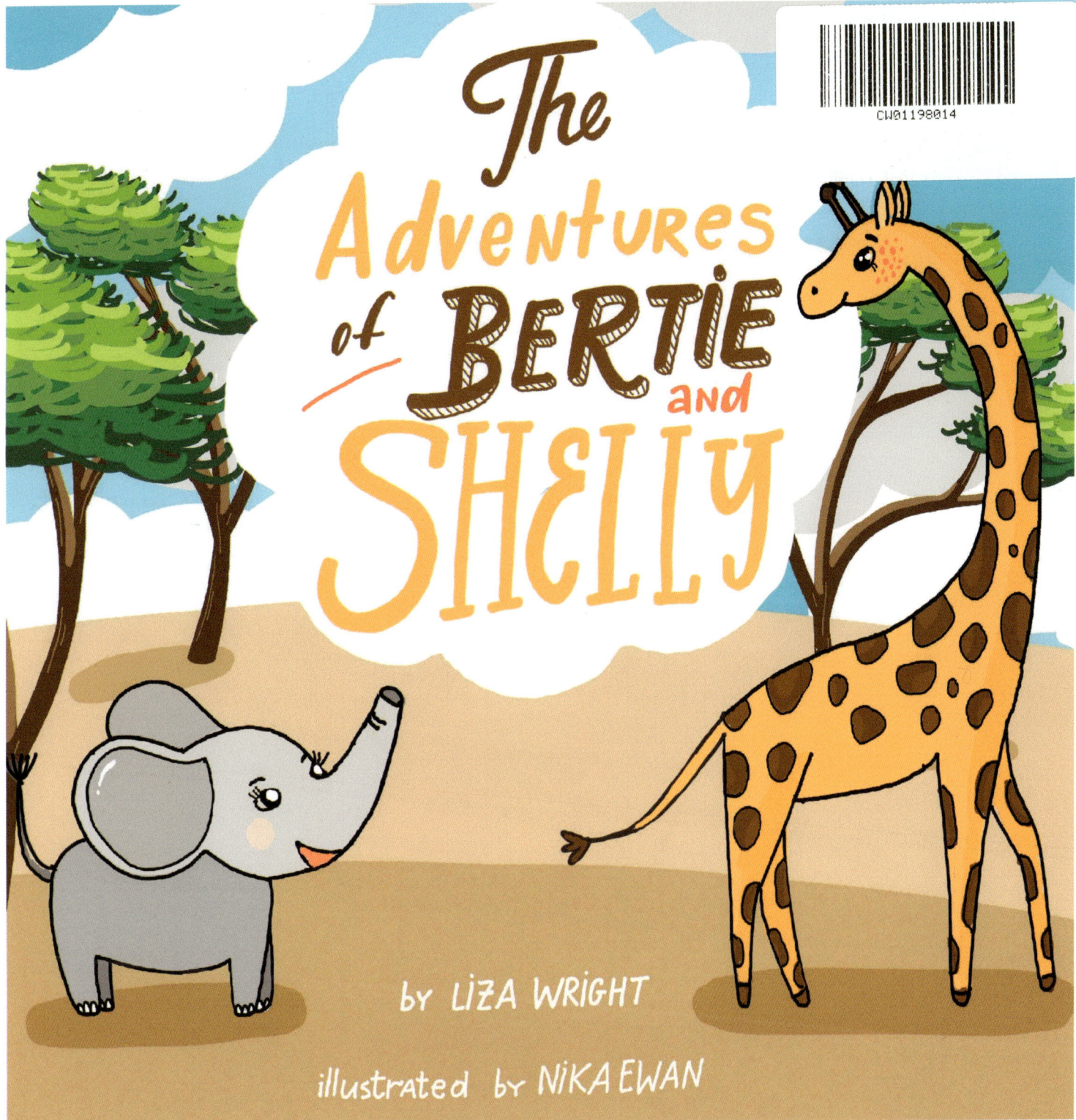

Somewhere in this vast land, there lived a giraffe.
It was very cheerful and friendly.
Somehow, plucking a leaf from the tree,
the giraffe saw a baby elephant.

But Bertie quickly outraced it and in a moment reached the target point. When the elephant reached Bertie it was very sweating to beat the heat. Shelly began flicking its ears to cool off.

"Bertie, let's go to the river!" Shelly said.
"Now is the time to freshen up."

When they came to the river, the elephant singsonged gaily, flopping down into the shallow, muddy water, rolling and splashing about, trumpeting and snorting.

Bertie went straight in and fall into water carefully.
After much hesitation, the giraffe decided to return to the ground.

"Shelly, the water here is very shallow. I can't bathe and playfully rolling around in the shallow water near the shore," Bertie said.

And... in just a moment... a crocodile lurched out of the water in the blink of an eye and clamped its jaws around the calf's trunk, gripping on tightly and pulling the victim into the river.

Against the odds, Bertie rushed to the friend to try to help him. It battled to save the helpless little calf from the attack and managed to shake off the reptile, which unclamped its jaws and stumbled backward eventually lurking into the murky water and letting Shelly go.

"You have such beautiful coloring and spot markings on the sleek skin. The spots add a glow to your skin in the sun." Shelly said. "Your tail is very long but my tail is too short."

"That's because you're young. As time goes by, your tail lengthens," Bertie said. "Is it just like yours?" Shelly asked.

So the friends went towards savanna trees, full of acacia and plants.
It felt like Bertie and Shelly had been in the tropical grassland forever when snatching at clumps of acacia leaves and stripping grass blades of their juicy parts.

Soon... The sun set on the horizon, Night came...

"Oh, it's too late, I have to go home to my mommy...

See you again tomorrow, Bertie!" Shelly said to its new friend.

Printed in Great Britain
by Amazon